The Map Maker

The Map Maker

An Illustrated Short Story
About How Each of Us Sees
the World Differently and Why
Objectivity is Just an Illusion

BRANDON ROYAL

Maven Publishing

Published by:

Maven Publishing
4520 Manilla Road
Calgary, Alberta, Canada T2G 4B7
www.mavenpublishing.com

Library and Archives Canada Cataloguing in Publication:

Royal, Brandon, author
The map maker : an illustrated short story about how each
of us sees the world differently and why objectivity is just an
illusion / Brandon Royal.

Short story.
Issued in print and electronic formats.

ISBN 978-1-897393-14-7 (paperback)
ISBN 978-1-897393-15-4 (ebook)

I. Title. PS8635.O953M36 2014
C813'.6   C2013-908168-2   C2013-908169-0

Cover design: George Foster, Fairfield, Iowa, USA

This story's cover text was set in Minion.
The interior text was set in Scala with section
headers set in Azuki.

Prologue

The Map Maker was by profession both a cartographer and a dealer in antique maps. In his spare time, when he wasn't working on commissioned maps or selling antique ones, he sketched and painted his own maps. The Map Maker had an unusual gift. By taking actual places and distorting geographical size, switching the locations of cities and countries, misspelling destinations, or putting new places on old maps and vice-versa, he created farcical representations that forced the viewer to think differently about geography and time. Just as striking were the vignettes he positioned at the corners of each map. These resembled incredible things—sea serpents, fearsome animals, mermaids, jeweled medallions, and strange artifacts. Many of the maps he created centered on Asia because he believed that, for most Westerners, this was the most exotic and mysterious of locales.

The Map Maker's "hobby" maps were in fact so striking that those who had the privilege of seeing them rarely made reference again to any of the antique maps for sale in his shop, regardless of how collectible they might be. For some peculiar reason, though, he would not sell any of his hobby maps or frame them for display, and instead left them rolled in cylinders to clutter the attic of his store.

The Map Maker's amiability and eccentricity complemented his graying hair and beard. Despite his extensive travel experience gained from having worked as a seaman in his early years, he rarely spoke of his experiences in detail, preferring oblique references such as: "Two coconuts equal one beer…dames with seaweed hair and olive eyes to match."

When I asked him about this, he replied curtly, "My stories are mine and better kept upstairs." He would then point to his head and follow with, "If people want stories they should get their own."

"Yes, but you experienced things in the days when they were truly exciting," I said.

"Nonsense," he snarled. "These *are* the good old days."

"You mean it's all relative?" I said.

"Things are never the way we imagine them to be. That's why—"

Off he went, leaving the floor of his shop and exiting via the storage room. In five minutes, which felt more like ten, he returned from the shop's attic carrying a huge wooden cylinder. He opened it and removed an enormous map. Attaching its top corners to a pair of hooks hanging from the ceiling, the Map Maker hoisted it into the air like a trophy fish being lifted from water. Imbued with vivid colors of blues and greens, golds and browns, the map stood as a magnificent, consuming sight.

"It's all islands!" I uttered.

"Most," he replied.

"The center island," I said, noting a small one with sun rays around it. "It looks like a pot of gold on a treasure map."

"That's Paradise Island."

"Is it—?"

"Point your finger at it," he interjected.

I moved my finger to within an inch of the map.

"Go ahead," he prodded.

As soon as my finger made contact with the map it began to glow and my finger pierced the surface as if it was invisible.

"Wha—?" I blurted, quickly pulling my hand back.

"Let your hand and arm go through. Walk through and you'll be in Paradise Island."

"Magic trick?"

The Map Maker did not respond to this question. "Keep this small map with you," he said, handing me what appeared to be an exact miniature version of the map before me. "When you want to return, you can use the point of a pencil to touch the gold dot marking the spot of Paradise Island. You'll be back here in an instant. Then you'll have some of your own stories to tell."

With a ceremonious chuckle, the Map Maker turned and left.

After a few minutes spent staring at the map and the hooks that held it, I reached out and pushed my hand and arm through the map. A flicker of glowing sunlight spread all around me. Then I stepped forward and pushed my face and body through just to see what was on the other side.

Truth Be Told

I had arrived in Paradise Island. I was standing before an outdoor patio and in front of me was a handwritten sign:

Movie Night
7:30 pm, Rashomon
**Black and white film
with English subtitles**

**"The subjectivity of truth and
the relativity of reality."**

The movie was about to begin. With people already seated in chairs near the front and center, I chose an aisle seat at the back and began to watch. The story opened with two men sitting in front of the ruins of an old temple, apparently taking refuge from the rain. They were mumbling to each other.

"I just don't understand," said the first man. "I've never heard such a strange story."

"War, earthquakes, winds, fire, famine, the plague...but I've never heard a story like this," said the second man, also obviously confused about the same event.

The story was about the rape of a Japanese woman and the death of her husband and the movie featured a series of flashbacks on four differing accounts of what actually happened on a forest road in twelfth-century Japan. Who is responsible for his death and what exactly has happened remains a mystery.

All we really know for sure is that the Japanese husband, dressed as a samurai and armed with a sword and bow and arrows, was escorting his wife through the forest. She rode high above the ground on a large, white horse, wearing white clothes and a sprawling bamboo hat, with a veil covering her face.

The film centers on the testimony of four individuals at the trial: the bandit, the noblewoman, the woodcutter, and the dead man, whose testimony is revealed to us by séance with the help of a shaman. As each person testifies, the movie uses flashbacks to replay each differing account of what happened. Here we are exposed to bizarre variations in viewpoint, all of which seem plausible.

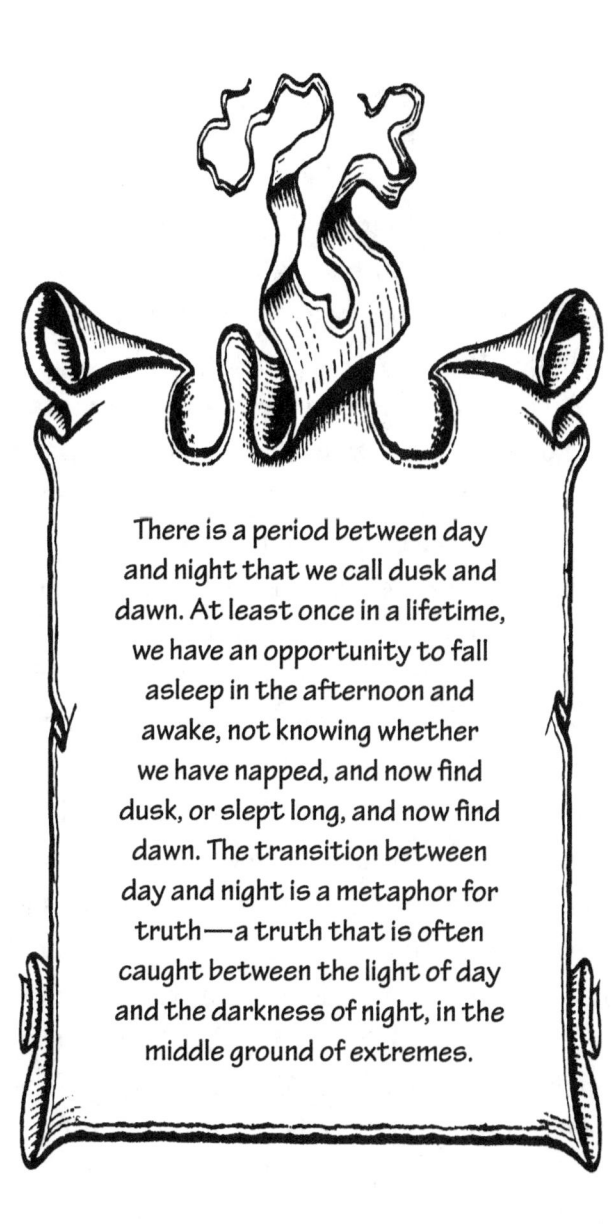

There is a period between day and night that we call dusk and dawn. At least once in a lifetime, we have an opportunity to fall asleep in the afternoon and awake, not knowing whether we have napped, and now find dusk, or slept long, and now find dawn. The transition between day and night is a metaphor for truth—a truth that is often caught between the light of day and the darkness of night, in the middle ground of extremes.

The bandit testifies first. As a result of being caught red-handed, in possession of the nobleman's horse, bow, and arrows, he knows that he is going to be killed regardless of what he says, so he claims to have no problem in telling the real story. With his roguish mannerism, the feisty bandit is unafraid to speak up, and his version of the story indeed seems credible.

According to the bandit, he was sleeping at the base of a tree, in the deadly heat of the summer afternoon, when the wife and husband passed by. A cool breeze swept through the trees, and just as it did, the lady's veil parted, and the bandit got a glimpse of how beautiful she was.

Having made up his mind that he wants this lady, he confronts the nobleman and tricks him into going for a hike into the forest to examine a stash of expensive swords that the bandit claims he hid and wants to sell. When the nobleman's back is turned, the bandit attacks him, wrestles him to the ground, and ties him up. The bandit then returns to find the woman who is waiting by a stream. He tells her that her husband was bitten by a snake and to come quickly. They charge through the forest and back up the hill. She arrives with a look of disbelief. How can her husband be sitting on the ground, tied up, and helpless? The bandit derives great joy from showing the woman how weak her husband is. Realizing her predicament, the woman pulls out a jeweled dagger and turns fierce, repeatedly trying to attack and stab the bandit. The bandit gleefully sidesteps these attacks. Eventually, the woman tires and he grabs the dagger and forces himself upon her. In this version of the story, she resists at first, but then succumbs to his advances. When it is over, the bandit is about to leave when, to his surprise, the woman yells out, "Wait! Stop!"

According to the bandit, the woman says, "Either you die or my husband dies. One of you must die. To have my shame known to two men is worse than dying. I will go with the survivor."

The bandit ponders these words for a moment and then makes the decision to cut the bonds of the nobleman, offer him a sword, and extend to him the chance for a final duel. After a long, tough sword battle, the bandit outmaneuvers and kills the husband. But by the time the battle ends, the woman is gone. In his confession at the trial, the bandit admits to having had his way with the woman and killing the husband, but denies wanting to kill the husband.

Next—the confession of the noblewoman. She also testifies before the same judge in an open court area. We never see the judge, but the camera makes us feel that we are viewing things from his perspective, so it feels as though each character who testifies is speaking directly to us. The woman weeps continuously as she explains a very different version of events. This flashback depicts the woman clearly struggling against the bandit. When her ordeal is over, the bandit runs off, leaving her to console her husband. While he is still tied up, she crawls over to embrace him. However, she is horrified at what she sees. Her husband's unbroken stare is glazed with cynicism and disdain, as if it's her fault. The scene portrays a man who has lost face and who wants to be held blameless, now that his possession has been sullied.

In this version, we feel compassion and pity for the woman, as she recounts her story: "Even now, when I think of his eyes, my blood turns cold in my veins. What I saw was neither anger nor sorrow, but a cold light, a look of loathing."

This most vivid scene of the movie has her repeating to her husband, "Don't, don't look at me like that…It's too cruel. Beat me, kill me, but don't look at me like that." She grabs the dagger and cuts him loose, offering him a dagger to strike her.

We are subjective creatures.
And our subjectivity both
protects us and blinds us.

"Now kill me," she admonishes.

She again begs him not to look at her that way. But he remains motionless with a fixed stare. This goes on for a few minutes. While he is locked in that same disdainful stare, she is in a fit of hysteria. After continuing to tell him not to look at her that way, she places the butt of the dagger at her throat and moves forward with the tip of the dagger pointing toward her husband. It would seem she is going to kill him by stabbing him in the throat. But that is all we see. Her memory fades and she tells the judge that she passed out and doesn't remember anything other than standing by the pond. She laments that she tried to kill herself several times but failed.

Next, the dead husband's spirit is summoned by séance and he speaks through the lips of the shaman. In this version of the story, his wife succumbs to the bandit and she actually becomes smitten with him. She urges the bandit to take her with him. The bandit is certainly willing to do this, except that the wife has a further demand.

"Please kill him," she urges.

The bandit is horrified at this request and throws her to the ground. Then he asks the husband, tied and sitting on the ground, if he should kill the wife at the husband's behest for suggesting such an act of betrayal. The bandit says to the husband that he only need nod yes or no. While the bandit is waiting for a response from the husband, the woman gets up and runs into the forest. The bandit chases her, and returns to tell the husband that she escaped. The bandit frees the husband and walks off, leaving the husband to stew in his own self-pity. The husband begins weeping and, upon seeing the dagger left on the ground by his wife, he picks it up and commits suicide by stabbing himself in the throat.

The final narrator is the woodcutter. He was walking in the woods at the time of the incident and apparently hid in the forest to watch events unfold. He claims that the wife was crying after the rape, and that the bandit, now smitten, begs the woman to be his wife and come away with him. In this flashback, the bandit appears very childlike. The woman refuses to accept the bandit's offer, runs to retrieve the dagger lying on the ground, and succeeds in cutting her husband free. Although now free, the husband apparently does not want his wife anymore, nor is he interested in attacking the bandit. The husband calls his wife a "shameless whore," only to have the bandit scold the husband for bullying his wife. As she continues to cry, lying in the middle ground between the two men, the bandit remarks, "Women are weak this way."

Then suddenly, the woman changes her composure, rising from the ground like a cobra, and becomes the intimidator. In front of both men, she tells them that they are pathetic. Then she laughs with a kind of cynical, hysterical, devious squeal.

"It is you who are weak," she says, addressing both of them in a raised voice. Turning to her husband: "If you are my husband, why don't you kill this man? Then you can tell me to kill myself. That's a real man."

Then she turns to the bandit. "When you told me you were the famous bandit Tajomaru, I stopped crying. I was sick of this tiresome daily farce. I thought Tajomaru might get me out of this. But you're just as weak as my husband."

Then she laughs again in that hysterical, devious squeal.

She continues: "Just remember. A woman loves a man who loves passionately. A man has to make a woman his by his sword."

These words send the two men into battle and after a long, brawl-like exchange, in which the men do as much wrestling as sword fighting, the

Objectivity requires two eyes: one to see, one to roam free.

bandit stabs the husband and emerges victorious. The noblewoman has disappeared and is nowhere to be found.

At the close of the movie, the two men who are seen at the beginning of the movie are again sitting waiting for the rain to end in order to go their separate ways. The movie ends without indicating to us what really happened. What version of this story was the correct one?

Never had I seen a movie that ended with such a degree of ambiguity. Usually movie endings exist to wrap things up. The strangest thing about this movie was that we have no reason to believe that any one of the four people lied. But how could four different versions of the story all be truthful?

The bandit claims to have killed the husband, in a sword fight, but insists that the woman forced him into doing it. The woman intimates that she might have killed her husband, but exonerates herself by embellishing her desperation and her husband's betrayal. According to the dead husband, he himself commits suicide, but his wife drove him to do it. And according to the woodcutter, the bandit killed the husband in a sword fight, but the woman instigated it.

I couldn't get that look of the wife's face out of my mind. In telling her version, she is gripped with that horrifying look on her face as a result of seeing the disdain on her husband's face after the rape: "One of you must die. To have my shame known to two men is worse than dying."

I sat for some time in wonderment. As I got up to leave the outdoor patio, I saw a lady sitting at a table at the opposite side of the exit. She had long, flowing white hair and the sign in front of her table read: "Destinies, spiritual guidance, relationships. Sage Sally. Inquiries welcome."

I noticed that her handwritten sign, with bright colors, was of the same style and script as the written sign that advertised the movie *Rashomon*. If she were the one who wrote that caption about the movie, she would certainly know what the caption meant.

I approached her and said, "I was just wondering if you—"

Before I could finish my sentence she asked, "So you'd like to know about the movie?"

"Yes," I said. "How did you know that?"

"You might say, that's part of my job."

I asked her about the handwritten caption that was scribed below the name of the film—the subjectivity of truth and the relativity of reality. "I think you wrote those words. I'm trying to figure out what they mean."

"There's an empty seat," she said, pointing to the chair directly in front of her table.

I sat down in the wooden chair that looked like it had been carved from a giant tree. It had knots in the wood and the arms of the chair looked like the gnarled branches of a tree.

"Subjectivity of truth, that's the easy part," she said. "We all see the world differently because we have different experiences. A woman who rides motorcycles thinks differently about motorcycles than a woman who doesn't ride motorcycles. A man who climbs mountains thinks differently about mountains than does a man who doesn't climb mountains."

I could barely contain my excitement as a result of running into, perhaps, the only person who could make sense of this movie. "So in the movie, the four people all perceived the event—the rape and murder—differently because they're not the same person."

"Something like that," Sage Sally said, pausing just long enough to sip from her bottle of water. "My take is that subjectivity of truth means that truth is some defined point or sharp line. And no one can find this true center. We all see things

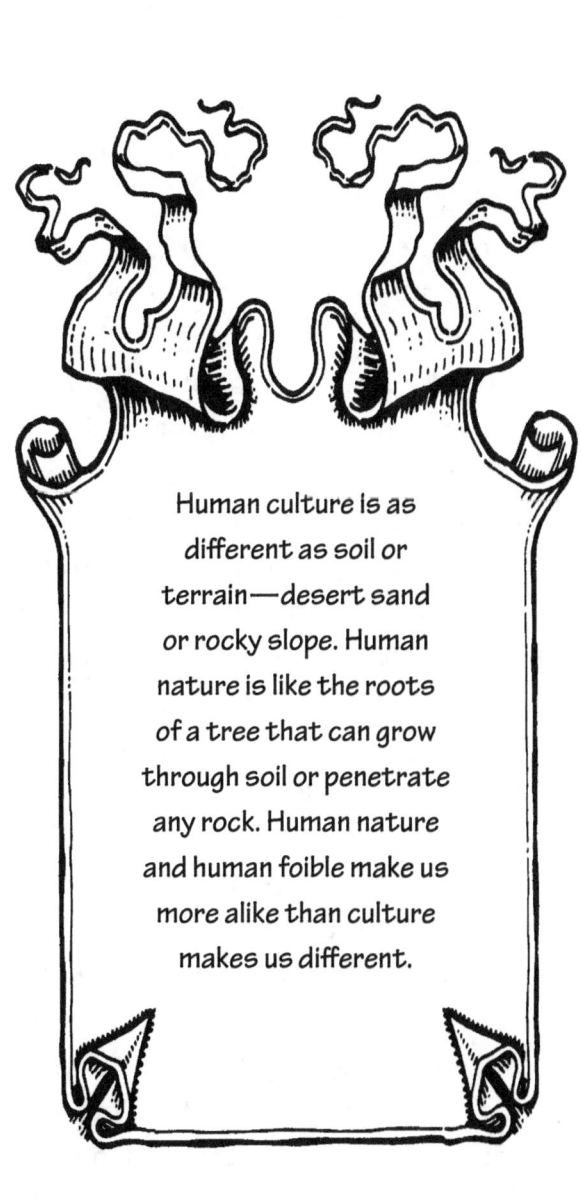

Human culture is as different as soil or terrain—desert sand or rocky slope. Human nature is like the roots of a tree that can grow through soil or penetrate any rock. Human nature and human foible make us more alike than culture makes us different.

differently, so our truth is usually skewed to one side of the actual truth."

"So for two people who are arguing, the truth usually lies in the middle between their two different points of view."

"I would agree with that," said Sage Sally.

"And by truth—this has nothing to do with religion, does it?"

"No, just perfect knowledge of an event."

"Think of it this way," she continued. "A girl is complaining to her friends that her boyfriend is an asshole. The guy is complaining to his buddies that his girlfriend is a bitch. Truth be known, more times than not, the answer is right in the middle, between these two viewpoints. I'm always amazed at how many girls believe their girlfriends, guys believe their buddies, and no one considers the middle ground."

After a few more moments of reflection, I pressed on. "So, I get the subjectivity of truth part, but what's the other part?"

"Relativity of reality. That's the harder part," Sage Sally parried. "In the movie, every character justifies his or her actions based on a belief of his or her reality. The bandit justifies his actions as if saying, 'Hey I'm a bandit, I'm supposed to rape and pillage, but I'm a good bandit. Sure I ıaped the woman, but I didn't bloody her. And yes, I killed the husband, but it was a fair fight and, besides, the woman forced me to do it.'

"The husband justifies his actions as if saying, 'I did look at her disdainfully, but I didn't harm her. I just looked at her. She's the one who sold me out, and that's why I killed myself.'

"The woman justifies her actions as if by saying, 'I was the victim of a crime. My husband no longer wanted me because of the shame we both suffered, so I had to kill him, because he wouldn't kill me himself.'

"The woodcutter justifies his view as if saying, 'Neither of the two men really needed to die, but they were forced into fighting each other to the death by the mere presence of a beautiful woman. She is their common enemy. That's also why I took the woman's jewel-studded dagger, which lay on the forest path, and which no one has been able to find.'"

"We justify our actions by who we are," I said, trying to see if I had hit the mark. "We reconcile our actions to fit the kind of person we think we are. We say, 'It must be the way I see it, because it really makes sense to me to see it that way. Maybe other people have different ideas, but mine makes perfect sense to me and, therefore, is as good as any other viewpoint.'"

"That's basically it."

"We use reality to justify our actions," I repeated.

"Yup."

"Makes sense," I said.

"Better make sense," Sage Sally said jokingly. "I made it up myself."

"So in reality, no one in the movie is lying. All are right and all are wrong!"

"That's what the movie's saying. There is actually no mystery. All the stories can be reconciled if you recognize the realities of everyone involved."

"Actually, I'm not sure if I really, really get it," I laughed. "But it sure sounds good."

"It's something that you can think about for years. Here's another way to think about it. Say you're passing by a shop on the street and you stop and look through the window. You see a clerk soaking and removing uncanceled postage stamps from some envelopes and you can see him gluing the postage stamps back onto a new envelope. Is this wrong?

"One person views this scene and thinks, 'Boy, that's a bit of work but it really shows

Words That Cannot Be Measured

appreciation
beauty, balance
cheer, compassion, cooperation
desire, deserving, destiny
effort, earnest, effervescence
faith, feelings, fondness, fairness
goodness, grace, greatness
hope, humor, heart, happiness
intuition, imagination, instinct
joy, jocundity, jest
knowledge, keenness, keepsake
laughter, loyalty, love, life, leadership
maturity, merriment, memorabilia
nostalgia, novelty, newness, nature
optimism, objectivity, omniscience
personality, patience, persistence
quixotic, quintessence
revelation, reason
sixth sense, satisfaction, serendipity
tenderness, time, togetherness
unity, universe, uniqueness
valor, vividness, vicissitude
wish, worthiness
xenial, Xanadu
yearning, Yin-Yang
zany, zeal

industriousness. That's the kind of person who gets ahead and ends up running a big organization some day.'

"Another person views this scene, and sees that very same person as one who would also be likely to steal paper and pencils from the company's stationery room. And if given enough opportunity, they're just the kind of person you'd hear about some day linked to an investment Ponzi scheme.

"And you can bet that if each of these two persons is asked why he or she feels the way they do about the person who reuses uncanceled postage stamps, each person will have a way to justify their beliefs. The first person will likely see the need to reward industrious behavior. Sure, reusing uncanceled postage stamps is technically wrong, but it's a small price to pay to help create a person who might go on to change the world.

"The second person will probably say that if something is dishonest or illegal, then it's dishonest or illegal, no matter how small the deed. If a person gets used to doing dishonest things, it could lead to other illegal things, and even encourage other people to do the same kinds of things."

"That's funny," I said.

"How could you get by in this world if you didn't believe that the way you see the world is basically the right way?"

Sage Sally continued: "The thing I find most interesting is that there is one word, and only one word, that every person believes they own. And that word is *objectivity*.

"No one really believes that he or she is the most handsome or beautiful, most intelligent, funniest, or most likable person. But almost everyone believes they're one of the most objective people they know."

"Why is that?" I queried.

"Ego and vanity," Sage Sally replied. "If you didn't have these words built into your system, you couldn't move forward in life."

"I don't think everyone sees themselves as having an ego or being vain."

"But it's still there. Just like rocks at the bottom of a river. You might not see them, but they're there."

"What about this?" I asked. "Even though the movie was set in twelfth-century Japan, what if we had a video camera that had captured what actually happened on that path in the forest?"

"Well, that would explain some things for sure. We would know for certain how the samurai husband died—did the bandit kill him, did he kill himself, or did the wife kill him? Pretty much everything else would still be open to interpretation."

"What!"

"That's what's really mind-boggling about the movie. It's saying that there can never be any absolute truth. Our earthly truth is only relative truth. As long as we see the world differently and justify our actions to fit our perception of reality, we will always have different versions of the truth.

"Sure, we'll be able to tell whether a law has been broken or whether a crime has been committed. These are man-made constructs. But we cannot tell real guilt or innocence or actual truth. These are relative concepts.

"As soon as we see or perceive something, it automatically makes 'truth' impossible. As long as we deal in reality, truth is rendered an impossibility."

"It really warps the brain," I said. "Subjectivity of truth means that we see things differently because we're different people with different backgrounds and experiences. Relativity of reality means that, based on our actions, we justify the things we do to fit the view of a person who sees the world like we do."

YOUTHFUL THREADS INTO THEMES

Nothing lasts, but nothing is lost. Nothing understood, but no meaning amiss. Quick, quack, nick, knack—schemes and dreams, youthful threads into themes. Sniff, snuff, scratch, dig—turn the ounces to screams, the pounds into dreams.

"It's a real trip taking all of this in at one shot," mused Sage Sally. "I'd say it requires either very little island punch or quite a lot."

Sage Sally looked as though she had spent many years living under the stars. Her face had many wrinkles, but they seemed to disappear beneath the glow of her smile. Determined to edge closer to the finish line of this amazing chat with Sage Sally, I offered a summary: "So in the end, truth isn't even in the middle ground of extremes, it's actually an illusion. Because we no longer know where that 'middle' is."

"Technically, well, that's right," she quipped. "When it comes to truth, we always start off seeing truth a little off-center—subjectivity of truth. That's because we're different people with different notions, ideas, experiences. And as soon as we go about completing actions based on those beliefs, we instinctively view 'that' line as being the center line of 'perfect' objectivity. This matches exactly our justification for why we do what we do—relativity of reality. Now we believe that our line of objectivity is, in fact, the true line of objectivity. Or certainly as true a line as anyone else's line."

Sage Sally had that special knack for boiling things down. There was something "unbreakable" about the way she understood things. I wondered whether this was something she learned from living on Paradise Island or was it knowledge that only certain people could tap into.

"We think we see the world objectively," I said, after a considerable pause. "But we don't and we can't. But if we could, would we rid ourselves of things like territorial disputes and wars?"

"Much of the conflict and destruction that we see around us is the result of the subjective way people view the events around them. Just think of all the fickle reasons that have caused people to go to war over the ages. If we could more easily see things from another person's point of view, a lot of intolerance and aggression would cease to exist."

"What if we could be totally objective. Wouldn't that mean that we would become robots?"

"That's a good point. If you think about what makes a person, that person, you realize that it's our tendency to see the world in our own way. Our thoughts influence our emotions and behavior. Our subjective way of viewing the world actually defines who we are."

"You're saying that we are defined by our subjective view of the world even though we want to be defined by our rational view of it."

"Pretty much. Think of what really makes you, you. You might say that it's your mind. But what is it about your mind that really defines you?"

"I'm not sure — achievements, personality?"

"For some people, like a well-known painter or singer, it could be a high achievement, such as a great painting or popular song. But one thing that defines each of us, regardless of whether we already have specific achievements, is our dreams and aspirations."

"So you're saying that subjectivity is a good thing?"

"Yes. It not only makes life interesting, but we have to view the world subjectively to keep our dreams alive. No one believes in your dream like you do. A dream is personal. And only you can protect it. If anyone attacks your dream, you have to be able to defend your dream against another person's ridicule."

"That makes sense. Some of the greatest human achievements were accomplished by dreamers. I'm sure they were all forced, at some point, to protect their dreams by refusing to listen to all the naysayers."

"Objectivity is needed to help you judge the events around you," Sage Sally said. "But it's not your objectivity that keeps you going. It's your subjectivity. Your passion."

"So objectivity is good and subjectivity is good?" I said, nodding in bewilderment.

"That sure seems to be the case. Real objectivity is impossible. Trying to be as objective as we can and seeing things from another person's point of view is very helpful in order to help us view events as accurately as possible. Seeing the world from our own subjective point of view is what makes us different and eventually defines us as individuals."

Sage Sally had introduced me to one of life's unsolvable riddles: How can we strive to be genuinely objective and wonderfully subjective—all at the right moments and in the right doses?

Epilogue

Soon I would leave Paradise Island. I would take the miniature map that I still held in my pocket, touch the gold dot, and walk back through the map to the spot where my journey began. But before I did, I reflected on the many things that had helped me to better understand the Map Maker.

The Map Maker was reluctant to talk about his travel or personal experiences because he felt it would rob others of their own experiences. Not only was he selective when it came to showing his map creations, he was also careful to let each person "determine" what the true value of a given map might be—a value that could only be measured in terms of how prepared a person was to receive a viewing.

That is why he would never sell his creative maps. They had no value and they had infinite value: They were the maps of human experience.

The Map Maker crafted vignettes, three or four per map, as if they were merely footnotes to an interesting story. He no doubt gained perverse satisfaction knowing that these vignettes would vie with the central illustration for the viewer's attention. So tantalizing in appearance, color, and strangeness were these vignettes that viewers would squint toward the corners of each map to get a better look, sometimes with jaw agape at what they saw.

He delighted in the prospect of a person facing the unexpected. I think this is why he created misrepresentations in his maps—to shock the viewer into acknowledging the possibility that things could be different from what they appeared to be.

Unlike his commissioned maps, which were exact, unequivocal, and explicit, his own creative maps were quixotic and open-ended. Striking and thought-provoking, his cartographic creations were neither too abstract nor too specific. This meant that the same person could see different things in them at different viewings.

The Map Maker loved the understated. I'm sure he liked being called "Map Maker" because it was an endearing veil he could hide behind. All the while, in his little "laboratory," he would ply away at his maps and then spring them on

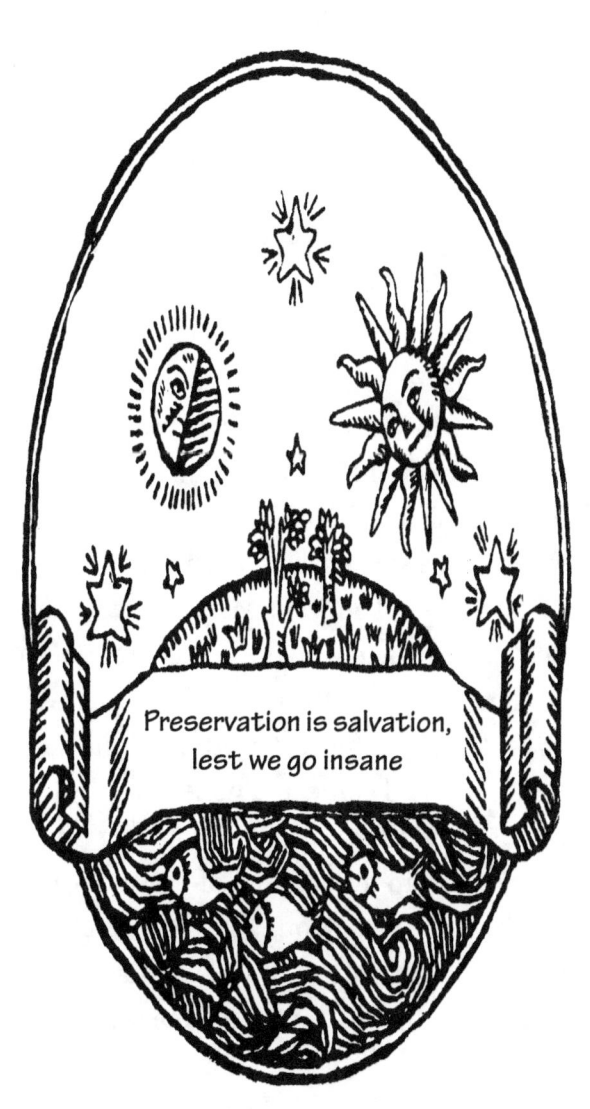

Preservation is salvation,
lest we go insane

the world, as if somehow unaware of the impact they would have. At his antique map shop, he met people from all walks of life. He seemed less interested in whether someone bought something from his shop than he was in the experience that a person had while visiting his shop. As long as each person found something of interest, that was what really mattered.

What did the Map Maker hate? I remember the Map Maker telling me about the death of a well-known customer. This was the story of a fellow who had finished first in the "big game"—finished school early, married early, had kids early, invested early, retired early, and now was first to die. The Map Maker hated hearing stories about people who died in the year of their retirement. Such was the fate of those who waited for the future to do those *other* things, only to find that their day had come and gone.

I long wondered why the Map Maker invested so much effort in the creation of his hobby maps, especially since he seldom showed them. I came to believe that his paintings and illustrations were a mechanism by which he vicariously relived his past journeys.

So many of his dreams were linked to travel, and he had traveled extensively to harvest these

Ode to a Manifesto

Our dreams, goals, and aspirations define who we are. A dream can never be objective. It is, by its very nature, subjective and uniquely our own and, therefore, requires our subjectivity to protect it. Our tendency to look at life subjectively is our defining characteristic.

Although we seek to be rational beings, we must embrace and celebrate our subjectivity and our innate and nurtured abilities to see the world differently. But being subjective does not mean being intolerant. Tolerant and passionate ... constructive, appreciative, and accountable ... seeking but sharing—this is how we must live our lives.

dreams. Now he wanted to ensure that his fondest memories remained untarnished. He knew that by never returning to the geographical location of his favorite travel vistas, he froze those memories in time. Never would he face the disappointment of returning to places that were only a shadow of their former selves, at least in his mind. The sketch that hung at the back of his shop—showcasing the sun, moon, stars, sea, and earth—was inscribed with a pivotal clue to the puzzle: "Preservation is salvation, lest we go insane." The Map Maker had aged believing that he could not survive without keeping his best memories alive.

The Map Maker liked to say that life was like an oyster and that dreams and memories are like pearls. Reality was the grit that got in the way, but it made everything possible. Indeed, it was the unwanted debris caught in an oyster's mouth that eventually creates its pearl. It was ironic that the very thing that the oyster didn't want, and would rather get rid of, was the very thing that created its most prized asset. In the same way that an oyster creates and protects its pearl, we too must create and protect our own dreams. We must let a little grit in, and nurture our dreams until they can take on a life of their own.

In the weeks and months that passed, I would again think about the "grit." Too little grit and our dreams and memories can't grow because they're not grounded. Too much grit and our dreams and memories choke and die. We are like an oyster and our dreams are like pearls. We have to let in a little "grit."

The Map Maker chose to remember the good times. For him, life's joys, happy thoughts, and novel accounts were worth celebrating. Despite the Map Maker's knack for plumbing the mysteries of culture and human nature, he was still able to see the lightheartedness in it all. And that is what I would remember and most admire about the man known as "The Map Maker."

We live to remember the good times. Our final, final thoughts will not be about the possessions we've amassed, but about the people, happy times, and novel experiences we've been fortunate enough to celebrate.

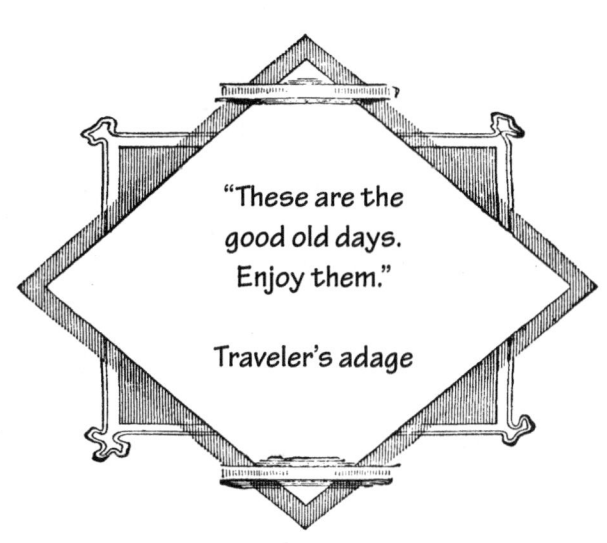

"These are the
good old days.
Enjoy them."

Traveler's adage

About the Author

Brandon Royal is an award-winning writer whose educational authorship includes *The Little Blue Reasoning Book, The Little Red Writing Book, The Little Gold Grammar Book,* and *The Little Green Math Book.* During his tenure working in Hong Kong for US-based Kaplan Educational Centers—a Washington Post subsidiary and the largest test-preparation organization in the world—Brandon honed his theories of teaching and education and developed a set of key learning "principles" to help define the basics of writing, grammar, math, and reasoning.

A Canadian by birth and graduate of the University of Chicago's Booth School of Business, his interest in writing began after completing fiction and script-writing courses at Harvard University. Since then he has authored a dozen books and reviews of his books have appeared in *Time Asia* magazine, *Publishers Weekly, Library Journal of America, Midwest Book Review, The Asian Review of Books, Choice Reviews Online, Asia Times Online,* and About.com.

Brandon is a five-time winner of the International Book Awards, a seven-time gold medalist at the President's Book Awards, as well as recipient of the "Educational Book of the Year" award as presented by the Book Publishers Association of Alberta. He continues to write and publish in the belief that there will always be a place for books that inspire, enlighten, and enrich.

To contact the author:
E-mail: contact@brandonroyal.com
Web site: www.brandonroyal.com

Books by Brandon Royal

The Little Red Writing Book:
  20 Powerful Principles for Clear and Effective Writing

The Little Gold Grammar Book:
  40 Powerful Rules for Clear and Correct Writing

The Little Red Writing Book Deluxe Edition:
  Two Winning Books in One, Writing plus Grammar

The Little Green Math Book:
  30 Powerful Principles for Building Math and Numeracy Skills

The Little Blue Reasoning Book:
  50 Powerful Principles for Clear and Effective Thinking

The Little Purple Probability Book:
  Master the Thinking Skills to Succeed in Basic Probability

Ace the GMAT:
  Master the GMAT in 40 Days

Dancing for Your Life:
  The True Story of Maria de la Torre and Her Secret Life in a Hong Kong Go-Go Bar

The Map Maker:
  An Illustrated Short Story About How Each of Us Sees the World Differently and Why Objectivity is Just an Illusion

Paradise Island:
  A Dreamer's Guide to the Life Lessons We Learn From Our Own Human Nature

www.ingramcontent.com/pod-product-compliance
Lightning Source LLC
Chambersburg PA
CBHW050912120626
46552CB00004B/1535